Text copyright © 2008 by Robin Pulver
Illustrations copyright © 2008 by Lynn Rowe Reed
All Rights Reserved
Printed and Bound in China
The artwork for this book was made with
acrylic paint on canvas.
The text typeface is Agenda Bold.
www.holidayhouse.com
First Edition
1 3 5 7 9 10 8 6 4 2

Library of Congress Cataloging-in-Publication Data
Pulver, Robin.
Silent letters loud and clear / by Robin Pulver ;
illustrated by Lynn Rowe Reed.—1st ed.
p. cm.
Summary: When Mr. Wright's students express a
dislike for silent letters, the offended letters decide
to teach them a lesson by going on strike.
ISBN-13: 978-0-8234-2127-5 (hardcover)
[1. English language—Phonetics—Fiction. 2. English
language—Spelling—Fiction. 3. Schools—Fiction.]
I. Reed, Lynn Rowe, ill. II. Title.
PZ7.P97325Sil 2008
[Fic]—dc22
2007016057

The publisher would like to thank Van Stone,
communication expert, and Dr. Hansun Zhang
Waring, Lecturer of Applied Linguistics at Teachers
College, Columbia University, for reviewing the
silent letters in this book.

Silent Letters

K   Knee, Knot

W   wrong, wrist,
    Mr. Wright

b   thumb, crumb

P   pterodactyl

Silent letters are seen, not heard.
They follow no rules when they appear
   in some words.
Watch for them and keep them in sight!
Your eyes, not your ears, must spell
   these words right.

Every day in Mr. Wright's classroom, without fuss or bother, the silent letters waited to take their positions in the spelling words.

They never called out, "Me, *me, me!*"

When it was their turn, they crept into their places without a sound.

SPELLING

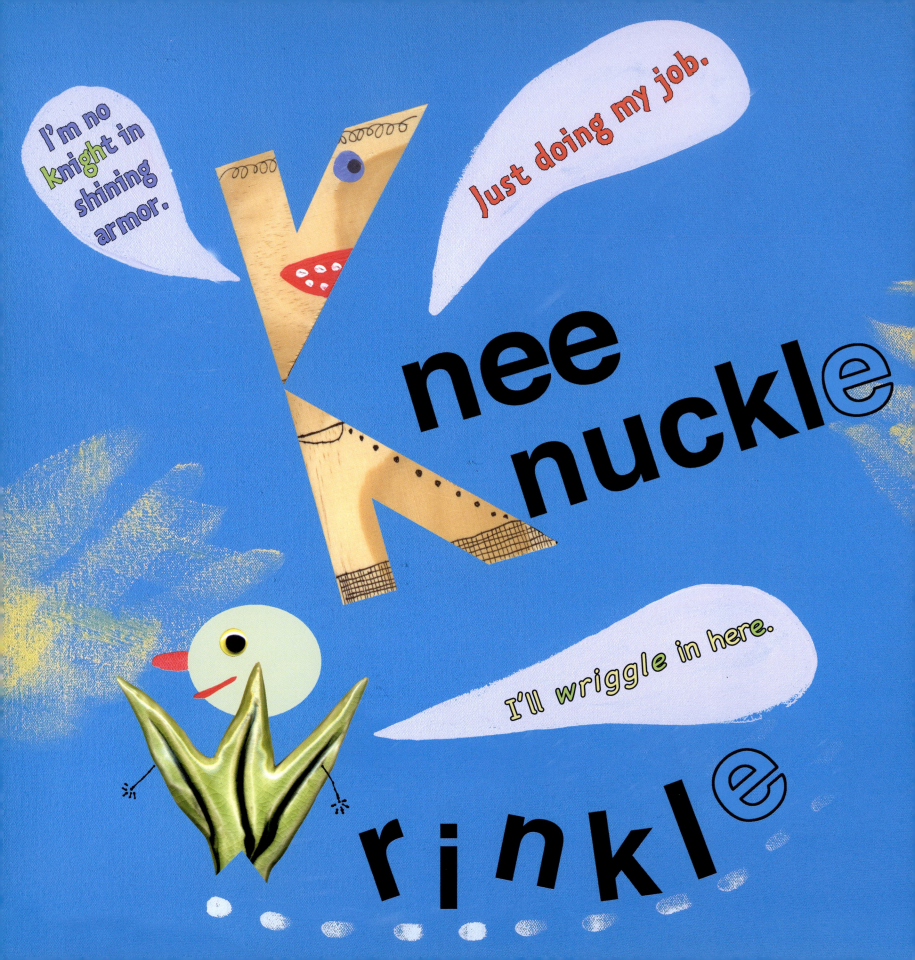

Often, silent e was chosen last.

One day, Mr. Wright checked his wristwatch. "That wraps up our spelling lesson," he said. "Remember, a mistake or two doesn't mean you're a bad speller. It means you've ALMOST spelled the word right!

Now, let's give a cheer for silent letters!"

The silent letters waited...

...but no cheer came.

The silence was deafening...

. . . until the kids started complaining.

"Mr. Wright, why do we have to use silent letters in spelling at all?"

We can't **HEAR** them!

Silent letters are a **PAIN!**

"Silent letters make spelling **too hard!**"

Silent
letters are
DUMB.

"If that's how you feel," said Mr. Wright, "you should send an e-mail to the newspaper. Make your opinions known!"

"Neat idea!" said the kids.

Cate sat down at the computer. The other kids helped her decide what to write.

Dear Editor:
  Mr. Wright says good spellers are made, not born. But we don't like silent letters! We can't hear them, so who needs them? Why use them? Silent letters should be banned.
  We hope you print this. We hope people will read it and agree that we are quite right.

  Hopefully yours,
  Mr. Wright's class

  P.S. Cate wrote this.

The silent letters were **dumb**founded.

**Silent
gh
sighed.**

"I thought
we were
important!"

"I know we are,"

muttered silent k.

"Now my stomach
is in knots."

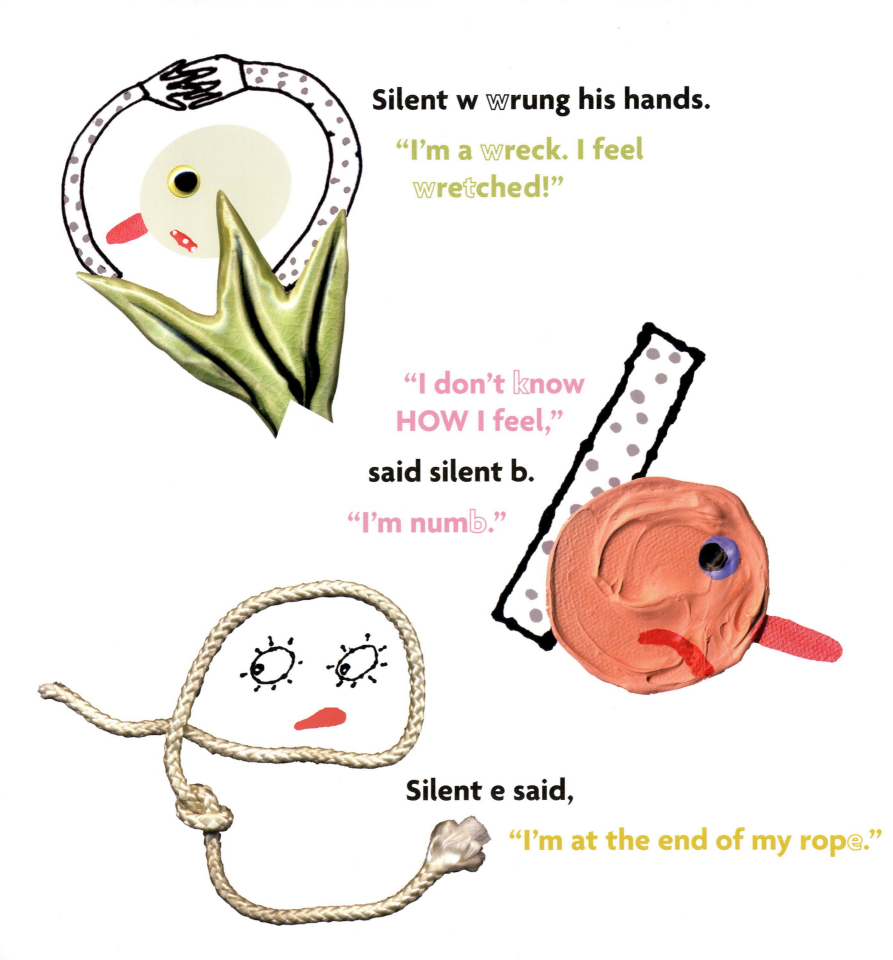

Silent w wrung his hands.

"I'm a wreck. I feel wretched!"

"I don't know HOW I feel," said silent b. "I'm numb."

Silent e said, "I'm at the end of my rope."

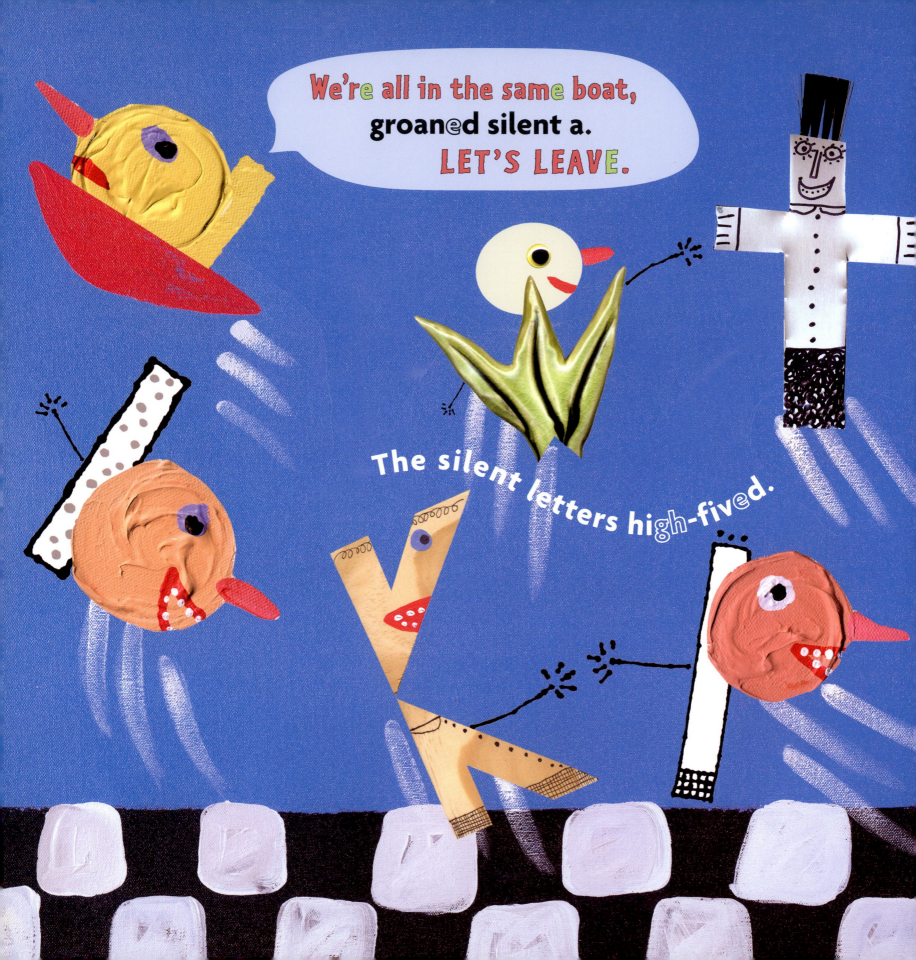

Just before Cate pressed Send, the silent letters sneaked out of the kids' e-mail.

Let's hide in the supply closet, said silent e. We'll be safe.

And out of sight, said silent gh. I've got a flashlight.

The silent letters nestled in the cavelike darkness.

Probably in the time of **knights** and **castles**.

The silent letters didn't want to suffer in silence anymore. They wanted to speak up for themselves. But how?

What could they do?

FIGHT
with all our might!

SCREAM
like in a bad
dream.

Bright
idea

But the silent letters had
to admit, they weren't the
fighting or screaming types.

Finally
silent g said,

"We could use
sign language!"

Everything they needed was right there in the supply closet.

The next day, Mr. Wright's class couldn't wait to check the newspaper. They opened right to the editorial page.

"Our letter! It's here!" shouted Joe.
"We're famous!"

The kids gave a cheer, loud and clear.

But when they started to read, it was the kids' turn to be silent.

Dear Editor:

Mr. rit says good spellers ar mad, not born. But we don't lik silent letters! We can't hear them, so ho needs them? Wy us them? Silent letters shoud be bannd.

We hop you print this. We hop peopl will read it and agree that we ar quit rit.

Hopfully yours,

Mr. rit's class

P.S. Cat rot this.

Finally, the kids got their voices back:

"What happened?"

"Somebody messed up our e-mail!"

"What's hopfully?"

"What's this about a bannd?"

"Who is Mr. rit?"

"Cat rot?!?"

"THIS LETTER IS EMBARRASSING!"

The kids were even more embarrassed when they read the editorial next to their letter.

HUH? WHAT...?
Fire Mr. Rit!

Of course good spellers are mad. So are we. Our readers don't have time to figure out messages with sloppy spelling. The only reason we're printing this letter is to highlight the spelling crisis in our schools.

—The Editors

The kids gathered around Mr. Wright, who was pale and sagging.

Suddenly the knob on the supply closet door turned. The door creaked open. Out marched the silent letters. They were carrying protest signs they had made.

They looked brave.

Silent letters are MIGHTY FINE (not mity fin)

Don't Knock Silent Letters

Silence is golden

Protect our right to remain silent.

Thumbs UP
for Silent
LETTERS!

Don't
leave
me
out

Don't
Write
us off!

"They're back!"
The kids
cheered, loud
and clear.

Mr. Wright
burst into
grateful tears.

Right away, with the help of silent letters, Mr. Wright's students wrote another letter to the editor.

WINNER OF THE GOLDEN PEN AWARD

(Best Letter of the Week)

Dear Editor,

Never fear. The future looks bright for spelling. We made peace with silent letters. We have learned to bravely face our mistakes.

Our teacher says the answer is . . . knuckle down and practice!!! As usual, Mr. Wright is right.

Your friends,

Mr. Wright's Kids and Silent Letters

Not perfect yet, but a brave try!
The quiet ones always surprise you.